Hello, Reader!

Once there was a bee
who sat on a duck.
"QUACK," said the duck.
"There's a bee on me."
The duck said, "SCAT!"
But the bee just sat.

You will like this funny story!

For my mother,
the one and only Bea.
— W.C.L.

Library of Congress Cataloging-in-Publication Data

Lewison, Wendy Cheyette.
    "Buzz," said the bee/by Wendy Cheyette Lewison; illustrated by Hans Wilhelm.
        p.   cm.—(Hello reader)
    "Level 1."
    Summary: As one animal sits on another in an accumulating progression, the reader learns the sounds each animal makes.
    ISBN 0-590-90741-7
    [1. Animal sounds—Fiction.] I. Wilhelm, Hans, 1945–   ill. II. Title. III. Series.
PZ7.L5884Bu   1992
[E]—dc20   91-19610
                                                                     CIP
                                                                     AC

36 35 34 33 32 31   9/9 0 1 2/0

Printed in the U.S.A.   23
First Scholastic printing, March 1992

BUZZZZZZZZ
Said the Bee

by Wendy Cheyette Lewison
Illustrated by Hans Wilhelm

Scholastic Inc. Cartwheel B·O·O·K·S

New York   Toronto   London   Auckland   Sydney

Once there was a bee who sat on a duck.

"QUACK," said the duck.
"There's a bee on me."
And the duck said, "Scat,"
but the bee just sat.

So the duck quacked again

and sat on a hen.

"CLUCK," said the hen.
"There's a duck on me."
And the hen said, "Scat,"
but the duck just sat.

So the hen danced a jig

and sat on a pig.

"OINK," said the pig.
"There's a hen on me."
And the pig said, "Scat,"
but the hen just sat.

So the pig took a bow

and sat on a cow.

"MOO," said the cow.
"There's a pig on me."
And the cow said, "Scat,"
but the pig just sat.

The cow began to weep

and sat on a sheep
who was fast asleep.

So the cow said, "MOO,"

and the pig said, "OINK,"

and the hen said, "CLUCK,"

and the duck said, "QUACK."

Then the bee said,
"BUZZ-Z-Z-Z!"

And that's all there was.